MR. WORRY

A STORY ABOUT OCD

Holly L. Niner

ILLUSTRATED BY **Greg Swearingen**

Albert Whitman & Company
Chicago, Illinois

To Evan for his courage, Beth for her understanding,

and Keith for his love and support—H L N

To Spencer, Hala, Rick, Kaye, Natalie, Rocky, and Felis—G S

Library of Congress Cataloging-in-Publication Data

Niner, Holly L.

Mr. Worry : a story about ocd / by Holly L. Niner ; illustrated by Greg Swearingen.

p. cm.

Summary: Eight-year-old Kevin is frustrated by his need to check things and repeat actions over and over until a counselor diagnoses obsessive-compulsive disorder (OCD) and teaches him ways to manage this condition.

Includes a note for parents and teachers explaining OCD.

[1. Obsessive-compulsive disorder–Fiction.] I. Title: Mister Worry.

II. Title: Story about obsessive-compulsive disorder.

III. Swearingen, Greg, ill. IV. Title.

PZ7.N62Mr 2004

[E]–dc22

2003016771

Text copyright © 2004 by Holly L. Niner

Illustrations copyright © 2004 by Greg Swearingen

Published in 2004 by Albert Whitman & Company

ISBN 978-0-8075-5182-0

Printed in China

10 9 8 7 6 NP 20 19 18 17 16

The design is by Carol Gildar.

For more information about Albert Whitman & Company, please visit our web site at www.albertwhitman.com.

Note to Parents and Teachers

Before being diagnosed with obsessive-compulsive disorder (OCD), my son wondered if he was crazy. He knew his thoughts and actions made no sense, and he wanted help. As parents we found his behaviors both heartbreaking and frustrating. When we realized that his problem was beyond our parental skills, we sought the help of professionals.

We learned that one out of one hundred children suffer from OCD. Research indicates that it is due to a chemical imbalance in the brain. A child with OCD is *not* crazy or seeking attention. Parents or an upsetting event do *not* cause OCD. Discipline, coaxing, or ridicule will *not* cure it.

People with OCD have recurrent thoughts or worries (obsessions). They develop repetitive behaviors or rituals (compulsions) to deal with the obsessions. Some common obsessions are germs, illness or injury, unlucky numbers or words, having things be "just right," or doing or thinking something bad. Common compulsions are hand-washing, constant counting, touching, doing things a certain number of times, checking things over and over, and asking the same question repeatedly.

For a child with OCD, the worries and rituals consume more and more time. A child lining up his trucks before bed may just be neat, but if he lines them up and then starts over and over again to get it just right, has to start over if he is interrupted, or says he can't sleep unless the trucks are lined up correctly, he may be more than neat.

There is hope for children with OCD. As in this story, cognitive behavior therapy (CBT) helps the child unlearn the compulsions that have developed. CBT alone or in conjunction with medication, which addresses the chemical imbalance, allows a child to regain control of his or her mind so that he or she can go on with the business of being a child.

Holly L. Niner

Kevin checked his closet. *Nothing in there.*
He pushed the door to make sure it was closed.
He pushed it one more time.

Kevin did a lot of things before he went to sleep.
He had to push the desk chair in until it touched the desk.
He made sure the books and papers were neat so they
wouldn't fall over. He lined up the cars on the shelf. His
mother had to tuck in his covers tight, like a cocoon.
He had questions to ask before she left the room.

"I did all my homework, right?"

"You know you did." Her hand was on the doorknob.
"Good night."

"I heard about someone with a tumor. I don't have one?"

"No. That's very rare." His mother sighed. "Better get
to sleep. I love you."

"I put all my stuff in my backpack, right?"

"What do you think?" his mother asked. "You need
some sleep. Good night."

Kevin heard his mother walking down the stairs. He leaned over the edge of the bed and looked. *No light.* He knew there wasn't a light under his bed — there were drawers there! But still, every night, his mind would get sweaty and he had to check over and over. He was afraid to tell anyone, even his mom and dad.

He snuggled under the covers and closed his eyes. He leaned over and checked for the light. A minute later he checked again for the light that he knew wasn't there.

When Kevin was at school, he had lots of questions to ask. Sometimes he already knew the answers, but his mind made him check.

"Turn in your homework," Mr. Westby said.

Kevin hesitated. "It goes in the blue basket, right?"

"You know where it goes." Mr. Westby wrote the homework assignments on the chalkboard.

Kevin put his paper in the basket. "The blue one?" he said again.

"Kevin." Mr. Westby turned from the chalkboard. "You know the answer to that question."

Easy for you to say, Kevin thought. *Your mind doesn't make you check over and over again.*

name <u>Kevin</u>

1. 6 x 24 =

2. 8 x 7

3. 10 x

4. 5 x

One day after school, Kevin and his mom were riding bikes. "Look at those beautiful flowers," his mom called.

Kevin didn't see the flowers. His mind was wondering if his mom might be an alien. He knew that wasn't possible. But *what if...?*

The trouble had started after he saw an alien on a TV show. He tried not to think about aliens, but he couldn't help it. He had to tell his mother.

"Mom, I know you aren't but sometimes—" Kevin started.

"What's the matter, honey?"

"Sometimes I wonder if you are an alien?" Kevin blurted out.

His mom stopped her bike. "Let's sit down and talk about this," she said. "You know I can't be an alien." His mother looked sad.

"I know," Kevin said. "But I start to think about it. What if you are? And you know what else? After you say goodnight, I have to check to see if there is a light under my bed."

"A light? But there are drawers under your bed."

"I know, but *what if.* If I don't look, my mind gets sweaty. I *have* to look, Mom." Kevin was scared. "I have to look over and over until I can fall asleep. Mom, do you think I'm crazy?"

"No, you aren't crazy. I *know* that." She gave him a hug. "But something's wrong. You shouldn't have so many worries. We'll find a way to help you. Remember how we got you glasses when you couldn't see the chalkboard?"

A few days later, Kevin's father took him out for ice cream. "Mom and I have been talking about your worries," his dad said.

Kevin played with his ice cream. "I wish I could just stop."

"We know," his dad said, "but you can't do it alone, so we've found a counselor to help. You'll go to see her."

"I'm scared," Kevin said. "She'll think I'm silly to worry about lights under my bed."

"She'll understand," Kevin's dad said. "She talks to people all day about their worries."

Kevin's parents were right. It was easy to talk to Dr. Fraser.

"Everyone worries," she told him, "but your brain is sending too many worry messages."

"Does that mean I'm crazy?"

"Not at all." Dr. Fraser smiled. "I think you have OCD—obsessive-compulsive disorder."

"What's that?" Kevin asked.

"OCD has to do with the way your brain handles doubts and fears." Dr. Fraser handed him her cordless phone. "It's like the OCD calls you with a worry message. Is there a light under the bed? Did you do your homework? And then it keeps pushing the redial button. Those messages are the obsessions and you worry about them. The compulsions are the things you do to try and stop the worries."

"You mean like when I check under the bed or ask too many questions?"

"Yes. You check things. Other people with OCD—"

"You mean other people are like me?"

"Many kids and adults have OCD," Dr. Fraser said. "Each one has a ritual, like checking, counting, or hand-washing to help them with their worries."

Kevin relaxed in his chair. He was glad to know he wasn't alone or crazy.

"When someone calls your house and it's the wrong number, what do you do?" asked Dr. Fraser.

"I say, 'You have the wrong number,' and I hang up," Kevin said.

"That's what you'll do with OCD. You'll learn how to hang up on the worry messages."

Kevin could picture the phone ringing. He'd hang up, but they'd call right back. His mind was sweaty just thinking about it. "I couldn't do that," he said.

"You can do it with help. I'd like you to take some medicine."

Kevin was surprised. "Why? I'm not sick."

"Do you like to run, Kevin?"

"I run races at school," Kevin said with a grin. "My teacher says I'm fast."

"Could you win the race if everyone had on shoes except you?"

Kevin laughed. "No way."

"The medicine will be your running shoes. I'll be your coach. We'll work on your racing strategy. Your family will be the fans. They'll cheer you on and remind you of the racing game plan."

"All right," said Kevin, but he wasn't sure about all this.

Kevin started his medication and met with Dr. Fraser every week. He picked a name for the OCD. *Mr. Worry.* He imagined Mr. Worry was a little man who kept track of Kevin's checking on his clipboard. Kevin was learning to hang up on Mr. Worry. If Mr. Worry called back, Kevin practiced saying, That's nonsense.

In a few weeks, Kevin was ready to tackle his bedtime routine. Each week he would stop doing one thing in his room. The first week it was the desk chair. At bedtime he did all his other checking and questioning, but he didn't move the chair.

"It's hard. My mind is getting sweaty. I think I should push in the chair," Kevin said. "What if I can't fall asleep?"

"That's Mr. Worry asking *what if.* Tell him you're in charge and you aren't going to listen to him," Mom said.

Kevin lay in bed for a few moments. "Hey, I feel better. I can leave the chair alone. Good night, Mom."

"Good night, Kevin."

Kevin did his other
checking, but he made it through
the week without pushing in his chair.

"What's your new assignment?" his mother asked the next week.

"No chair and no straightening things on the desk." Kevin sighed.
"This will take forever."

"You did great last week," his mother said.

Kevin straightened the cars on the shelf. "But I'm going to try
to do it faster. Tonight I won't close the closet door or look for the
light, either."

"Are you sure?"

"Yes." Kevin hopped into bed and asked his nightly questions.

After his mother left, Kevin heard Mr. Worry. *What about the
light? The closet? The desk? The chair?* He just couldn't stand it.
He had to get up and check them all.

After that Kevin took things one step at a time, like Dr. Fraser had said. After a few months, he could stop doing his bedtime checking.

One night he thought, *This is easy. Mr. Worry is gone.* He spent the next day at a friend's house. They watched a scary movie and played the Revenge of the Aliens video game. That night Kevin checked his closet three times and looked for the light.

Mr. Worry was calling again. Kevin told him, "Don't call back because I won't be watching scary movies for a long time."

Kevin had calls from Mr. Worry if he was too tired or too busy. One week it was the science project he was behind in because he forgot to write down when it was due. Another time he went to two sleepover parties the same weekend. He was too tired to hang up when Mr. Worry called.

Kevin learned that he had to help the medicine if he wanted to keep Mr. Worry from calling. When Kevin ran or rode his bike he could feel himself getting strong— strong enough to hang up on Mr. Worry. Finally he could fall into bed and go to sleep like everyone else.

"I'm proud of you," Dr. Fraser said. "Your teachers report fewer questions at school. You're going to sleep without checking."

"I feel great. Should I keep coming to see you?" Kevin asked.

"You're winning the race, but this is a marathon," Dr. Fraser said. "You can come less often, but I still need to see you."

"That's good." Kevin was glad he was winning, and that he could still talk with Dr. Fraser.

"What do you do when Mr. Worry calls?"
Dr. Fraser asked.
  "I tell him, That's nonsense. Then I say,
Don't call again, because you're not in charge. *I* am."